BUNNY TRICKS

Bunny Tricks

Dark Maid Sehseh Vol 3

Sarah Elliot

Katrina Allcroft, Boo Lai

Sarah Elliot Author

CONTENTS

Thank Yous 1
   1 - Mistress Kani 2
   2 - Planning 9
   3 - Why We Are So Naughty? 16
   4 - Twenty To One 25
   5 - Goo Bunnies 36
   6 - Creative Team 44

THANK YOUS

Author - Sarah

Thanks for everyones continued support over the course of this work and for engaging with the story constantly.

As always big hugs and loves to my parents, friends, collegaues and everyone else who has said that they want more of this crazy work. Always makes me smile

Co-Author - Kurt

I want to thank my Mam, who found it funny that a story thought up between me and my best friend during a boring quarantine was going to actually get put forward to a release but she sadly never got to see it actually happen.

We love you Sandra, hope you're getting to read this wherever you ended up

1

MISTRESS KANI

A young lady watched the world go by from her window, staring with dark brown eyes that blinked curiously. The curtains moved in the light breeze, and a smile occasionally flickered onto her face, framed by long, neatly braided black hair, set with silver threads and charms. She looked to be in her early twenties and seemed prim and proper in her wheelchair. She wore a long black pleated skirt, with a white shirt and a silk cardigan with white trimmings. A choker sat around her neck, set with a pendant of a purple rabbit. The young woman made no movement, other than the slightest of expressions, and it was easy to presume that she was someone trapped within her own mind.

But Irene Kani was not like anything many people had seen, and she planned to keep it that way. Even the recent passing of her father wasn't something that couldn't be overcome, although it did throw a spanner in the works of her plan. Her mind buzzed with ideas, running over possible scenarios, and checking them against databases, whilst double checking some recent analytics for a little project. It largely ran itself, but Irene had always thought it was best to keep a close eye on Project #74968 whenever the opportunity presented itself.

Small glitches and moments were one thing, but if that girl started to remember too quickly, then the plan would go to hell in a handbasket. To be fair, there were times when it was pretty much already there, but Irene liked to try and keep in control of everything whenever possible.

The door to the reading room opened and a male figure in a tailored suit walked in. He looked every bit the part of a classic Battle Butler, except perhaps for the long hair which was looped around his head to make it appear that he had two large rabbit ears.

"Good evening, Mistress Kani."

"You look like fan art of a certain character, but I can't decide which one," Kani said, giggling through the neurological link that was shared between the pair of them. "You could have at least changed your hairstyle."

"But then I'll blend in far too well and that'll just be boring," the Butler replied, pouting just a little.

Kani let out a sigh. "The whole point is to blend in: to not be noticeable for any reason other than the bloody obvious you nit. If this is to work, we must stick to the plan."

"That's already out of the window."

"Ralph, I don't have time to argue with you over this," Kani snapped, wishing that she could shake her head, but her physical body would not permit it in the slightest. "If she gets so much as a glimmer of recognition off you tonight, it's going to trigger the programs early and we can't have that."

Ralph sighed and shook his head. "She'll be fine, she didn't recognise me when we met at Alvin's truck."

Sighing again, Kani stared at Ralph. "That was different. She was preoccupied and you barely saw her for a minute. You know what she's like, and if she starts remembering, it's going to overload her. We can't have that happen until the upload is complete."

"You were against this upload until your father died," Ralph retorted, but he also reached for a brush to start working on his hair.

Kani was silent. Her eyes continued to stare at the same spot, but there was a little glassiness to them to suggest tears. It was one of the many curses that she had to live with. Whereas her mind was free to explore and experiment and engage in all manner of activities, Kani's physical body was restricted in everything. Even when she connected to her own Specialist Model to help with the fight, Kani temporarily lost part of herself and never fully got to experience what it was like to have a body. To be able to move freely, to speak, to hold, to touch, and everything else that everyone always took for granted.

Placing down the brush, Ralph moved over to the still figure and wrapped himself around her in a hug, sighing deeply. "I'm sorry, that was mean of me."

A hiccup sounded through the link before Kani released a long sigh. "It's fine. I'm still getting used to the thought. Though I'm glad that he put a contingency plan in place for this... almost like he knew."

"He probably did," Ralph replied, grimacing a little at the words as he pulled back, "He was always ahead of the game, even before we were properly playing it."

A brief hum came from the girl then she was silent once again, but Ralph was used to this. When she was sad, Kani would quietly busy herself with some tasks and indicate when she was ready to be disturbed. So, Ralph took it upon himself to gently wheel the girl out of the reading room to prepare for the evening ahead. The funeral wake should have been a sombre celebration of the achievements of Kani's father, but both of them knew that it was going to turn into a shit storm. If it wasn't due to the appearance of family, which would inevitably cause conflict as there were too many money-grabbing hands trying to secure themselves onto the vast wealth and research of Rabbit Enterprises, then the political side would take offence when a certain announcement was made, which would seriously invalidate any work of Phoenixolutions.

Though, if truth be told, Ralph was rather hoping for the latter once Sehseh and Rhain turned up. As long as everything went according to plan, which, as the untimely death of Mr Vidyut had proved, wasn't what was going to happen in the slightest.

Ralph made sure to wash and dress Kani into more fashionable mourning wear, as even a paraplegic girl had to look the part in this crazy-ass world. Once he was happy with her, he started to head towards the main lounge, where the guests would start to assemble, and thankfully did not jump out of his skin when Kani suddenly asked, "What was it like, seeing her again?"

"Strange," Ralph replied, mulling his feelings over for a few seconds. "I knew who she was, but it was like looking at her from a different angle. So much changed and different but still the same."

"Hmm, I know what you mean," Kani replied, "It is strange but she's still there, somewhere beneath all of her current peppiness."

"I think she was peppy until the monster took everything from her," Ralph replied, then chuckled, "She never hung out with us before that."

Again, Kani did not reply for a few seconds, but Ralph did not blame her in the slightest. Talking about the past was hard. People said that it got better with time, but few had survived what they had, and even then, it was questionable how much of them had survived. Whilst there were memories that the pair of them shared, it was sometimes hard to work out what was real and what had been fabricated or replaced. Especially after Mr Wirth had scrambled them both so strongly in an attempt to get rid of their existence, like rabbits that kept on breeding no matter what the farmer did.

"You sent the files to Sunny, right?" Kani asked, suddenly very business orientated.

Ralph nodded, "Yes, she relayed the plan to Rhain and Alvin, and the files were uploaded. Though, I warn you, your cousin is not best pleased with the route that we are taking."

A chuckle came from Kani. "Oh, I know. He worries far too much but then again...that's what love does to you."

"I suppose," Ralph replied bitterly.

"Don't throw a huff over this again," Kani said, "You know fine well that it was one-sided, and she told you a million times not to. But you never did listen, did you?"

A snort came her way from Ralph, "You do realise that she ditched you for me, right?"

"She did not," Kani replied, "What we had wasn't anything like you thought. We knew the rules and we stick by them."

"Says the biggest rule breaker ever," Ralph teased back with a smile.

Kani did not reply, instead focusing on splitting her mind in two as she began connecting to the Special Unit which she operated. "True," she mused ever so slightly and then chuckled, "But I don't have a choice in the matter any longer. Besides, I'm still her bestest best friend ever."

Ralph glared at his charge, but gently patted the girl on the head as he secured the wheelchair in place on a balcony above the main room, somewhere where they could observe everyone but not be noticed unless someone happened to actually take a moment to look up. He cast his eyes around the grand room which was beginning to fill with people, noting faces and IDs as well as tracking the number of personal bodyguards, Maids and Butlers who were entering along with their masters.

A shudder went through his system as he spotted a couple of heavy females and for a moment, he narrowed his vision down on a pair of young-looking schoolgirls who seemed to be entirely out of place.

However, they both disappeared from sight almost immediately, almost as if they had detected his stares and that raised suspicion. Pressing a device on his wrist that looked like a watch, Ralph narrowed his field of vision to where he had last seen the two. "Randal, scan through recognition software and identify those intruders. Iris, I think we have infiltrators. I'll get the security drones working, but..."

"Already spotted them," Iris replied, calm and with her voice like rich chocolate, "They're two kittens who should not be here but they're with Mrs. Vidyut, so for now, we'll have to leave them alone. I'll ensure that our little bunny goes nowhere near them unless absolutely required."

Ralph nodded, "Thank you, keep me updated."

"I will do," Iris replied, stepping away from her charging point and heading towards the main doors, watching as people and maids alike stepped out of her way whilst she just politely smiled towards them. It wasn't every day that a Special Classification Model walked in front of you, and Iris was famed for being one of the absolute best ones ever made.

Then out of nowhere, a figure launched herself at Iris with a cry of "GLOMP!"

2

PLANNING

Seaton Delaval Hall was a grand old building, with large pillars adorning the front entranceway steps and the imposing structures of a bygone age were captivating. The Hall was unique in being one of the only pre-nuclear-age buildings that was still standing and maintained its ancient outward appearance. The stones and mortar could have probably told a history longer than that of any families that were alive today and it screamed of the potential power that the recently dead occupier could have wielded.

However, the late Mr Vidyut wasn't a man who appeared to actively seek power, or money or fame. He was something of an old relic himself. An oddity who had grown up in a time that seemed just a little too advanced for him, yet somehow, he had slotted in almost perfectly.

Rhain shivered a little as he stared up at the massive structure after leaving the safety of the car, flanked immediately by Sehseh who was eyeing the security guards carefully. There was a sombre feeling to the air, as expected for a funeral wake, and everyone was dressed in appropriate mourning clothes. Rhain was in a black suit, his hair slicked back and gloves covering his fingers, whereas Sehseh was in a rather plain and simple black long-sleeved dress that went down to her ankles. Her plaits cascaded gently down her back, and her smart black shoes made her look more mature than usual. This was somewhat ruined by her bunny backpack, but of course Sehseh wouldn't be anywhere without it. It was a look that didn't suit her, but she blended in almost perfectly with the other maids and butlers who were present.

Many pairs of eyes turned their way as they entered, their stares a complicated mixture of judgement, accusation, disbelief, jealousy, and rage. Rhain ignored them all and instead headed into the main hall.

"There are a lot of people here," Sehseh commented, following in step. "Lots of others like me."

"Most will just be bodyguards," Rhain replied, keeping his voice low. "Perfectly natural for a function such as this."

"Too many," Sehseh said, blinking slowly as she looked around. "I count at least two per guest. I think there's some kittens too?"

Rhain snapped his head towards her in a warning glare, and felt a shudder go through his system at her returning look. While he was aware of things not exactly being right with Sehseh tonight, he didn't have to be happy about it. The plan that he was basically being forced to go through with was too risky, too direct and would throw them straight into the spotlight he was trying to avoid. Rhain, unlike his uncle, didn't want to be outed yet as an active campaigner against Mr Wirth, at least not publicly. It was apparent that other forces needed to be taken into consideration. Rhain was also a much more recognisable target and in the public eye would have more of a reason to actively try to oppose Mr Wirth. Even if he wasn't fully prepared for the public to know of that reason yet.

Sehseh smiled softly at Rhain and made a face imitating a cat, accompanying the expression with a 'meow' that dissolved into giggles. Rhain shook his head and turned away from the sniggering girl.

"Sehseh, we are at a funeral, we're supposed to be respecting the dead."

"No one here cares about the dead though," Sehseh replied, pouting a little, "Well, maybe you and a few others, but you'd cry at a butterfly's funeral, Master Rhain."

Catching hold of Sehseh's arm to tug her into a small alcove that presented itself, Rhain glared at his Maid. Taking a few deep breaths, he managed to bite down on the growing anger that was building up in his head before he snapped and said the wrong thing. "You need to cool off, Sehseh."

"No, I..." Sehseh started, then trailed off, blinking, and snapping her head back and forth with a sickening sound of metal and flesh working against one another. She rubbed at the base of her neck. "Hmm, that's odd. My overheat shouldn't be kicking in yet. Alvin said it would be in approximately three hours."

"I did tell you that this plan was stupid," Rhain said in a low hiss. "I'm sending you back home. This is not going to work."

Sehseh immediately shook her head. "I'm not leaving you undefended here. Too many threats."

"I can't use you if you burn out on me," Rhain said softly.

"And you won't get what you want if you're dead," Sehseh replied, then pulled back a little and shook her head. For a moment she looked scared and very much alone, but then she straightened up and nodded her head rather stiffly.

Rhain straightened up too and turned to find himself looking at another man, around the same height and age as him. The man wore a black suit with a diamond studded tie and held an air of sophistication about him that was not to be messed with. With his light brown coloured hair, grey glassy eyes and a fake tan that looked almost natural if it weren't for a few streaks that hadn't been corrected properly, Rhain recognised him immediately. Behind the man was a Heavy Butler, who looked out of place in the suit that he had been forced into with a mop of white hair and an expression of a boulder. He would have looked far more natural in a posing pouch on a Mr Universe contest than standing behind Philip Vidyut, ex-bastard son of the late Mr Vidyut and a friend of Rhain's from their school days.

"Hello Philip," Rhain said politely, offering his hand, "I would say it's a pleasure to see you but given the circumstances…"

"Cut the formalities with me, Rhain, I don't need anyone else reminding me of what the old git has probably done to me," Philip said, returning the handshake, nevertheless. "I'm just glad I got my own company underway before all this came to light. Would hate to think what the under scum would have done to me given half the chance."

Rhain blinked. "You're not upset about it all then?"

"Was bloody raging mate, when I first found out," Philip replied, but then shrugged casually. "But then I got to thinking, and realised that maybe he gave me the best way out of a whole lotta shit. Most o' the bastards here tonight are just money grabbing whores anyway. I don't know why half o' them even think they have the chance of being the heir to his work."

Rhain chose his next words carefully. "So, you don't know who the heir is?"

"Nah, no one does." Philip shrugged. "I don't even think his Special knows. If she does, then it's locked under a very secure file with a password that no one would be able to break. Not that I would try to get into her brain… her boobs maybe but…"

"He's ninety per cent intoxicated, Master," Sehseh muttered, her voice low.

Philip seemed to notice her for the first time and looked confused for a second before suddenly grinning. "Oh, your little project! I virtually didn't recognise her in the slightest. Ha, you even managed to reconstruct her face. That looks so good, almost a hundred per cent like the original!"

"Philip," Rhain said in a warning tone, catching hold of the man's hands as they strayed towards Sehseh's face. "I think you've had a little too much to drink."

"I need a lot of drink to get through this shit, Rhain. But you've done a cracking job on her, I'd say. Ha, I bet if that old, twisted sod was standing here right now, he wouldn't be able to recognise her in the slightest." He snorted, then swayed and turned to face Rhain straight on. "I'm curious though. How did you get her past security? Even if she's mostly rebuilt with all the technology they have, she's still got that chip from him in her! Vidyut hated anything to do with-"

The thought was interrupted as Philip suddenly paused, hiccupped loudly and then vomited all over Rhain. He stopped for a second, but before Rhain could step back, Philip opened his mouth again and more puke came out, ruining every piece of clothing that Rhain was wearing. Thankfully his glasses were saved, but that was about the only good thing in this entire sorry episode.

Sehseh looked as though she was about one second away from bursting into giggles but pulled out a handkerchief instead. "Shall I help you clean up, Master?"

A new voice cut through the scene, soft, sincere and like that of cut crystal. "There is a room free in the guest suite, with an appropriate bathroom and I can easily get you a new suit downloaded digitally, Master Rhain,"

Standing just a little back from the group was a tall lady with an hourglass figure that was alluring as it was striking. She had soft, honey coloured skin and her blond hair was tied up in a couple of high ponytails but with enough fringe falling over the eyes to make her appear enticing and mysterious. She had smoky grey eyes, soft red lips and a face that was designed to evoke the image of an angel.

She wore a simple, dark blue dress with a pinafore, both going down to her knees, where you could just about see that her white thigh high socks had little stars on the tops to keep them up. She had a solid gold collar around her neck and two silver bangles around her wrists, signifying her as a Special. The Maid smiled and bowed politely. "I will have Mr Philip escorted to his own private wing to recover."

"Thank you, Iris," Rhain said, stepping neatly away from Philip as his Heavy started to drag him away.

Iris bowed but suddenly snapped her head to the side just as Sehseh yelled out, "GLOMP!" and threw herself at the other Maid. Clearly anticipating this, Iris easily held her ground, catching Sehseh and hugging her back with a grin.

"It's good to see you too, Sehseh."

"It's been too long!" Sehseh pouted. "And I have so much to tell you, Iris, and…"

Sehseh twitched suddenly, codes flashing across her eyes, before she turned and stared out across the room. There were many guests filtering into their assigned seats, each one dressed immaculately in their finest business suits and all of their Maids and Butlers dressed just as finely. For a moment, her eyes drifted up towards a discreet balcony, then a flash of static turned her attention back to a podium in the centre of the room where a hologram projection was showing.

"Sehseh?" Iris asked, stepping closer. "What's wrong?"

For a full thirty seconds Sehseh did not respond, seemingly distracted by something across the room. It was only when Iris placed her hand on the Sehseh's arm that she snapped out of it and turned to stare at her. Iris looked concerned. "Do you need access to a booth? I have one of the finest in the master's quarters."

Shaking her head rapidly, Sehseh let out a breath. "No. I should be fine."

"Are you sure about that?" Iris asked, her voice becoming lower with each passing word. "You're not yourself tonight, Sehseh."

Sehseh looked away again, this time focusing on two girls in school uniforms that did not match with anyone other than the apparent schoolmaster that was with them. She didn't respond to Iris at first, then suddenly started. She turned to Iris and nodded. "I think a booth may be... just what... wait..."

"This way," Iris said, indicating to one of the staff to come and help Rhain. "I think it's for the best."

Rhain, still covered in vomit, watched as Iris began to lead his Maid away, then brought out his PDA, checking the encrypted message to Alvin that contained the login to the network. He glanced up briefly at the balcony where Sehseh had looked moments earlier. Noting that two figures were present, he sent a nod their way before graciously following the staff members to a private part of the house. He was sure that things were going to get very interesting in the next few minutes and whilst part of him wanted them to be there, he also knew that being safely out of the way was also going to be a very good idea.

3

WHY WE ARE SO NAUGHTY?

Stepping out of the shower and finding a new suit waiting for him, Rhain instinctively turned towards the window, expecting Sehseh to be standing there wearing the smile that she only reserved for him. Instead, he jumped out of his skin when he found Iris standing looking at him instead.

"Geez, give me a heart attack, why don't you?"

"Sorry," Iris replied, smiling gently. "I just came to inform you that Sehseh has been hooked up and is safely secured on the network."

For a few long seconds Rhain paused, then shook his head. "I still think this is a stupid plan."

"We know and we understand," Iris replied. "But trust us, your Sehseh will not be damaged by this. She is protected far better than you know."

Rhain snorted. "By a psychotic computer program who happens to be in love with her, supposedly."

"Do I detect a hint of jealousy there?" Iris asked.

For a long few seconds, Rhain glared at the Maid before huffing. "Don't do that to me when I'm not talking to you. It's creepy."

Raising an elegant eyebrow, Iris chuckled. "Yes, you are jealous. Even though she would give up everything for you."

"He would take her away from me if he got half the chance and you know it," Rhain retorted, finishing putting the new suit on and noting that it had extra body armour built into it. "I'm allowed to be concerned about that."

"I know you are, my dear cousin," Iris replied. "It's just so sweet for me to see. Especially when she tells me all about how much she adores her Mr Fox."

"Irene!" Rhain snapped at the girl inside the Maid. "Go bug your cohort and stop trying to distract me from stressing out. I want Sehseh out of here before all hell breaks loose down there and I hate that I've agreed to this stupid plan."

"It's not a stupid plan, that's why you agreed to it," Iris replied, smiling, and blinking her eyes three times to return them to the more usual settings. "Master Rhain, the announcement will begin soon. I will be next to you to act as security, while Sehseh is connected and broadcasting."

Blowing out a long breath of air, Rhain shook his head again. "This isn't going to work. There's too many imposters and those two kittens-"

"Will be dealt with," Iris finished, stepping closer. "Don't think we didn't plan for every eventuality. Now come, stop being such a worrywart and let's see how the old man would play his little trick."

The pair walked down the stairs to the main central room and took their assigned seats. For the first time in a long while, Rhain felt uneasy. He wanted nothing more than to step back into the shadows and be unobserved, but with all the security passes and unlimited access he had been granted, it was impossible not to notice that virtually everyone was setting their targets on him.

He really wished that Sehseh was beside him. As much as he appreciated Iris, it just wasn't the same. Iris had more protective functions than Sehseh, but she really belonged to his cousin and her creations, not to him. That made him even more nervous, which made him automatically want to be out of this whole god damn situation even more.

Rhain turned to Iris and quietly whispered, "Is she going to be okay?"

"I think so," Iris replied. "She was able to log on fine, so I'm pretty sure that everything in the network is being monitored and sorted out correctly."

Rhain stared levelly at the Special. "You do know what the network would like to do to her if it gets half the chance, right?"

Iris nodded, "I was informed. But the access portal she is going through is hard to get through at the best of times, even for the likes of your Sunny."

"How can you be so sure of that?" Rhain asked lowering his voice a little.

"Because it is *my* access point, one that requires extra special authorisation to even see and three levels of interconnected passwords from myself alone to even start it up," Iris replied, her voice just barely above a whisper. "The network knows not to mess with that access point. Master Vidyut ensured that it would be forever safe and tamper proof. Only two people have ever tried to access it and the only reason one of them was successful was because Master Vidyut had a soft spot for Alvin. Even then he clipped him around the ear."

For a second Rhain was silent, his mind buzzing with hundreds upon hundreds of thoughts before he narrowed his eyes slightly. "I just don't know why he's playing this game. You are more than successful and have practically run the company for all these years. The public would accept you."

"A paraplegic in a wheelchair who controls everything with her mind. The public would freak out and Mr Wirth would just use it as an excuse to finally finish obtaining everything." Iris smiled softly. "You're still sweetly naïve to the world at large, but I suppose it makes the most sense in the end. Just take a moment and breathe, life is about to get a bit more exciting for you."

Frustration welled up in Rhain's heart, but he was distracted by his PDA flashing up a series of messages from Alvin and Sunny, informing him that the plan was underway and that several armed units were heading in their direction. Alvin had also sent a document with the original guest list and then a second one which had been updated, and Rhain felt his stomach sink to the floor. There were twenty known contacts of Mr Wirth or Phoenixolutions and all of them had brought their own personal Battle Maids, Butlers or Heavies with them.

Rhain turned to Iris, "You expect her to go twenty to two?"

"One," Iris whispered back, not looking at Rhain. "I'll be busy setting up the outer defences for the PMC who are on route to us."

Before Rhain could even open his mouth in surprise, there came a chiming of a bell, and Rhain focused his attention back to the front of the lavishly decorated room. From the central pedestal, the holographic projector turned on and produced a 3D image of the former Mr Vidyut. He was a man of average height, with white hair and a smartly trimmed beard, in a brown suit with patches that displayed nothing of the wealth he truly possessed. However, there was a glimmer in his eyes, one that made him appear to be a man possessed with an idea. Rhain felt a shiver go through his body, remembering vaguely that his uncle only ever looked like that when he knew that he had found something out that would make him a winner.

"Good evening, ladies and gentlemen." Mr Vidyut spoke in the soothing tones of someone who had lived a very long and full life. "I thank you for coming to my funeral, as I know this is the only time that these words will ever be allowed to be spoken aloud. Many of you will be here for the purpose of finding out who my real heir is and seeing if you can take them out, and I wish you the best of luck. My heir has been working in the shadows for a long time and has many outlets that will make it impossible to stop her grand influence over the markets. My nephew, Rhain, is also heavily involved with my work and he shall become the vice chairman of the company, even if he would rather that office fell to someone else."

Rhain got the distinct impression that his uncle was looking directly at him at that moment, and a frown crossed his face. His uncle had always had a particularly odd sense of humour and seemed intent on making life as awkward as possible. It was no wonder that Sehseh and the others had agreed to this crazy plan because the world would focus on him rather than the real threat.

"For those of you still wondering, and just to clear it officially, my heir is my daughter, Kani Irene. She officially takes over my company as of tonight, though has been running things far better than I have for a very long time. She is a rebel with a cause, who overstepped the boundaries and did not return from her self-set mission to expose the cruel reality of the Battle Maid and Butler program." Mr Vidyut paused for a second and then smiled softly. "Now, though, she has an outlet for exposing that, and in time, you will all come to learn the truth. Especially with the advancements in the neurological technology that we have made together over the last few years."

Rabbit Enterprises was a company that specialised in neurological development for medical and scientific purposes, working on the relationship of the human mind and how its electronic pulses could be separated and used to operate several different sources. There were several different companies who produced the work, but Rabbit was the best known due to the immense research that they had conducted, specifically around medical research to assist those who had been injured or born with defects. The Impulse Drive, which allowed the human brain to be connected to a series of computers and run multiple functions, had first been developed by Rabbit Enterprises before being copied by Phoenixolutions. But whereas the latter company had turned it into a billion dollar enterprise to make life easier for a busy CEO and his cohorts, Rabbit had focused the technology into a more practical and accessible function of being able to assist those in society who needed it without damaging them further. The Nightingale Company worked with Rabbit to get the technology working with all sorts of different people, and ever since the first successful connection between a human mind and a specially made Maid body, the speed of development had increased dramatically. The company was worth trillions alone on that technology, but it was guarded and secured and only released to those who needed it the most.

Rhain smiled to himself for a moment, glad to know that Kani was now partially out in the open, and he was proud to serve alongside her. The feeling faded quickly when he remembered that there were at least twenty potential assassins and two kittens all targeting him, but Mr Vidyut started talking again and distracted him from his worried thoughts.

"Now, I move onto the main reason that I brought you all here tonight, knowing fine well that there will only be a handful of you who will survive." He paused for effect, then continued. "As many of you are aware, I have always held a strong dislike of Mr Wirth, the best producer of Battle Maids and Butlers this side of the last World War that saw our planet virtually ripped in two. 'Dislike' is an inadequate word, but since there are ladies present, I shall continue to remain as polite as I possibly can. I have refused to work with him, to acknowledge his presence at high class affairs, and I have deliberately barred him from attending my funeral. I've also barred any of his associates or products even though I am fully aware that there will be several cats lurking around here, but my security team have already tagged you so don't get any ideas. There have been many excuses given of course, but now that I am no longer among the living, I can safely say these words aloud."

A smile crossed Mr Vidyut's holographic face.

"Mr Wirth is nothing short of a murdering bastard who takes innocent children from their parents and turns them into his beautiful creations with a hidden flip trip switch, which allows him to take control of them regardless of any other programming, at any time that he deems it necessary to do so. I don't know how many lives he has ruined using this chip or how many innocents he has caused the death of, but with the data that is now transmitting across the network through a specially selected Maid... I am more than sure that his private military contractors will already be descending onto the house to eliminate the data and at least half of you, if you are not quick enough to get a move on."

The old man smiled calmly, like a grandfather who had just sentenced his least favourite grandchildren to their deaths. "One last note before you all start running about like headless chickens. I want you to pause for a few seconds and take stock. Some of you gathered here today have a reason to dislike, hate, or want to get rid of Mr Wirth and his terrible organisation.

You have next to no ties to him in any general classification, and other than formal functions, you would rather curse his name than exchange pleasantries with him. For those that applies to, I have sent copies of this information to a secure file on your networks and I'm sure that you'll be most fascinated by what you read. As for the rest of you, who are here under orders to steal the data or kill Rhain and any mentioned heirs, I'll say to you now...goodbye and good luck."

As soon as he finished speaking, vents in the room opened up and Rhain found himself being pulled to the floor with a breathing mask over his face. For a few seconds, he didn't know what was going on, then he heard bodies hitting the floor as a heavy gas started to fill the room. He turned to glance at Iris, who shook her head at him and covered his eyes with his hand. He didn't know how long he was down, but the sound of a few dull shots had him stiffening up.

Suddenly, the pressure was off his body, and he was being hauled upright into a standing position. Iris was lying still and stiff on the floor where she had been protecting him. He didn't have a chance to let out a yell as he found a gun being pushed under his chin by one of the schoolgirl assassins. He figured that the other schoolgirl must be the one behind him, holding him in a very strong grip. "You should learn to look more closely," the first girl said sweetly, orange hair tied up in two neat little buns. "You were so easy to..."

Something clattered onto the ground not far away from the trio and as they looked over, it turned out to be a large red bunny shaped button. It lay still for a second before standing upright, and the bunny blinked.

"What the hell?" said the girl with the gun.

"Baba boom!" was the button's response, in a high-pitched squeaky voice. "Baba boom! Baba boom! Baba boom! BOOM!"

The button suddenly shot up into the air and then landed, only this time with an explosion that flared straight through the room. Rhain found himself being knocked to the floor once again, on top of Iris's body and for a moment he was sure that everything was going to end.

Then a soft kiss was placed just under his ear and Sehseh spoke gently. "There's only twenty of them. You just stay under Iris whilst she resets, and I'll take care of everything else."

Once she was sure that the light was gone, Sehseh stood up slowly and glanced around. The entire room was a mess of concrete and several scorch marks from emergency escape hatches and jump systems. A few decoy bodies lay scattered around, while the only other survivors were the twenty Maids and Butlers who had been accompanying those of a questionable nature. All of them now had a red code flashing across their eyes: 1011.5 Kill Code.

"Permission to activate Protocol 1?" Sehseh asked.

Hiding further under Iris in the hopes of not having to witness the destruction, which was about to rain all around him, Rhain stammered out an answer.

"Granted."

4

TWENTY TO ONE

A fist came towards Sehseh, but she blocked it with ease and twisted the girl's arm, forcing her back before swinging around to strike her in the side with a sharp kick. In response, the Battle Maid stumbled to the side, then punched towards Sehseh's gut, a blade shooting out which pierced the skin of her lower rib cage, but Sehseh merely grabbed her wrist, twisted it out of her body and forced it back into the other girl's eye, sending her screeching backwards into the nearest wall. A knee to the head stopped the infuriating noise.

Two more jumped her from behind at the same time. A male grabbing hold of her throat whilst a female kicked out her legs and they attempted to floor her in order to shatter her spine. Sehseh shot her fingers out towards the female's eyes, gouging them out with her sharp nails, then dug her elbow into the male's side to knock the wind out of him, but he held grimly on. Gaining purchase on the floor, Sehseh propelled her body upwards and over the man, dragging him down and slamming a hand into his throat.

A kick to her chest sent her backwards, but she was quick to flip herself upright and counter-blocked the series of knife thrusts that were coming her way. This new girl was quick and clearly programmed to be a swift killer. Sehseh felt the bite of the blade as it struck her already-injured arm. Biting back a curse, she quickly kneed the girl in the stomach, elbowed her in the back of the head and re-slammed her head back onto her knee just to make sure that the Battle Maid would stay down and not bother her.

She ripped the knife out of her arm, pausing long enough to notice that it was actually a letter opener, before hurling it straight into the throat of a male who was charging at her with the remains of a table. Sehseh quickly sidestepped as the figure crashed down, grabbing onto the table leg to wrench it free and slam it into the face of another Butler who was charging at her. He fell hard and fast but swung his legs out underneath himself to catch her own and send her tumbling to the ground. Sehseh barely got a chance to react when another Butler attacked her, attempting to stab her chest with a broken bottle but letting out a surprised sound when it slipped harmlessly off.

"Best armor around." Sehseh smirked and punched the guy in the face, grabbing the bottle and slamming it into his own exposed chest, then kicking the one who had knocked her to the ground in the balls with a crunch that suggested he wouldn't be pleasing his mistress anytime soon. Quickly, she was back on her feet, ducking a feather duster which had been flung towards her, and twisting it away before the concealed blade could flip out. Instead of striking her, it flashed into the neck of a charging Battle Maid and cleanly beheaded her. A spurt of blood cascaded over Sehseh's face, and she hissed at momentarily being blinded.

The Maid with the feather duster wasted no time in striking with her weapon in repeated jabs, forcing Sehseh back into the clutches of another Butler who got her into a body lock. The Maid with the duster smirked as she struck out towards Sehseh's face and head, clearly trying to dislodge the electric neurons in her mind to render her helpless. On the fourth blow, Sehseh just giggled like a schoolgirl and grinned towards the stunned maid. "Clearly you don't know who I am."

A sharp kick to the Butler's instep with her kitten heels had him caught off guard before Sehseh slammed her elbow into his stomach, followed by a fist to his nose and her foot to his balls before she pushed forward, taking a bite out of the other Maid's neck and tearing a chunk out of it. They crashed to the floor together, and Sehseh slammed herself down extra hard before using the momentum to push herself back up, smash the Butler's teeth in and then roundhouse kick another Maid who was coming her way.

Being off balance, she crashed to the floor again, but was able to grab hold of the duster, swinging the blade around into the face of the Butler with the broken teeth then thrusting forward to slice the other Maid in two. She dug the point of the blade into the other Maid's head to cut off the sensors like she had been trying to do to Sehseh. She then spiraled around, gutting the Butler who had held her, and thoughtfully brushed his escaping organs back into his stomach with the feathers.

Another Butler got her in a back lock, but this one swung her around and away, passing her to a group of three Maids who may have been toys in a previous incarnation or part of someone's fetish, as Sehseh found herself being suffocated by the biggest pair of breasts that she had ever felt. They were so big and comfortable that Sehseh momentarily felt the desire to squeeze them and snuggle up securely, until a sickening squelch brought her back. One of the girl's finger nails had extended out into six inch claws and dug straight into her stomach. Sehseh yelped and pulled back, finding herself temporarily locked as her body tried to register and counteract the anomaly of the pain that was coursing through her system.

There was a dire medical warning in her lower left-hand vision, and Sehseh knew that she had to get out of this situation as quickly as possible. Snapping her head right and then left, she allowed the medical override to inject her body with the adrenaline she needed to keep going, and added a small injection of STIM to the mix. It was something that she hated using, as whilst it gave her a boost to her physical and mental aptitude, it would slow down her automatic healing processes. It also gave her a god complex with a horrendous comedown, but she had to serve her Master, and this was the extra little boost she needed to win the game.

With a roar, she kicked out at the girl with the big breasts, twisted herself around in the hold of the one with the nail claws, and headbutted the second one cleanly. She grabbed her clawed hands, pulled her back in for another headbutt, then slammed her own nails into her throat. A punch to her head caused her to sidestep but she swung the girl's hand towards the Butler, catching him on the face and then roundhouse kicked another Maid who was coming towards them. A glint of steel caught her eye, and Sehseh ducked a grapple attack from the big breasted Maid and the Butler with the ripped-up face. She charged towards the last girl.

The last girl held an army knife, which she must have grabbed from one of the dust bunnies who had fled at the first sign of real danger. Sehseh wasted no time in knocking her to the floor, slamming her head sharply against the unresisting concrete several times in rapid succession with a splattering of blood, before grabbing the blade and turning to slam it into the leg of the Butler with the cut up face. She dragged it upwards, cutting him from thigh to gullet as she rose and pushed him back into the rapidly approaching big breasted girl to make them both fall back.

Quickly she leapt over, smiling sweetly at the Battle Maid as she slipped the blade into her throat. "I'll be nice to you, because your pillows were lovely."

A gurgle was her reply before a kamikaze scream alerted her to yet another approaching Maid, and she turned just in time to block the katana which was coming her way. She pushed back, forcing the Maid back a few steps, then charged forward and ducked a swipe which would have sliced her head open. She struck at the woman's stomach and pushed her back. The Maid's eyes were a bright green from the STIM shots she must have thrown into her body, and Sehseh rapidly back tracked as the Maid came charging back at her with a series of strikes that left no room for counterattack, only retreat. Sehseh was forced to move quickly. The blood stained floor was becoming slippery and Sehseh paid the price when her foot slipped through a small pile of entrails and the katana blade landed in her shoulder. However, Sehseh quickly regained her stance and pushed herself forward, ignoring the steel that was cutting through her shoulder to get a clean stab at the other girl's heart. A second stab went to the throat followed by a third to the eye.

She pushed the fallen body away, pulled the katana out of her shoulder, and threw it like a dagger towards one of the remaining Battle Butlers who had been waiting on the side-lines with a pair of nun chucks in his hands. He was impaled against wall with the handle just resting on the bridge of his nose.

The final three all looked to be High Class Models and Sehseh smirked. The High Classes were a step above the normal Battle Maids and Butlers, but not quite the strength and versatility of a Special Class. They couldn't be readily customized, and generally they were as ugly as the day they were finished being turned into their Status. They were tanks, built with muscles and capabilities which were designed to be imposing and heavy on the eye, the type that would have been described as meathead bodyguards in the past. Their downfall was that they only really acted as protocol dictated and were therefore easy to predict. Though, as Sehseh knew, they were still pretty hard fuckers to take down, as pain just didn't register with them.

"Ladies first," Sehseh said in a happy sing-song voice, a blooming smile on her face.

The first High Class Butler stepped forward, his fists the size of two legs of lamb, and he swung a punch towards Sehseh. She naturally ducked the first punch but took a slam from the left hand side that cracked at least two of her rib bones. In fact, she was pretty sure that one of them was broken into several pieces. Ignoring it, she grabbed hold of the hand which had struck her and flipped herself upwards in a spiral to get a firm leg lock around the man's thick neck. She tightened her grip as she continued to twist around and felt more than heard the satisfying snap as his neck couldn't withstand the pressure.

She allowed them to fall together, rolling out of the way as she took a quick moment of respite behind an upturned table to catch her breath. She sent another quick shot of STIM through her system and then laughed gleefully when a bin was upended onto her head. For a few seconds, she was completely blinded and could not move her upper body, but instead she just giggled like a school child and shouted, "Look, Master, I'm a robot!"

Unaware of anything else that was going on around her, Sehseh ran around in a circle making silly beep beep noises before careening straight into the High Class Butler and butting his head with the edge of the bin. Her fingers were quick to find purchase on the rim as she kept bashing into him, pushing the bin upright each time as she pulled back so she could see what she was doing.

Over time, she turned the bin from a cylindrical tube into a flat blade, as the man's mass was next to impossible to believe. With each strike, the edges became harder and harder until at last there was a firm solid corner which she slammed repeatedly into the larger man's form, giving him no time to react and counter her moves.

She only stopped when one of his eyeballs popped. She dropped the bin to the ground, only to be blown back across the room as she was hit firmly in the chest with a shot gun pellet.

Sehseh slammed hard against a wall and slid down it, breathing heavily and for the first time in a while finding herself unable to really react. The High Class that approached her now was huge, her form that of a female body builder and yet she still somehow managed to look pretty. She reminded Sehseh of those female knights you saw, the ones who lead the battles across the Hybrid Lands and were famed as being untouchable by anyone. She quite liked them and smiled at the comparison.

"You're pretty," she sang pleasantly towards the High Class. "I wouldn't have chosen you to be the one but I'm happy."

"You're not dead yet," the High Class replied, loading another shot into her gun, her voice deep and calculating. "I'd normally give you the option to let you witness your master's death, but after this little display, I think that would be a bad idea."

Sehseh flicked her eyes up to her master who was standing in the hidden balcony, a glass of scotch in his hand and just a smattering of blood on his collar. He nodded, holding up a small pen drive in his hand and the Battle Maid couldn't help but grin a little.

She turned her attention back to the High Class. "Afraid to say you've lost, pretty one."

The High Class snorted. "Like I care. Orders are orders and you're on the kill list."

The shot gun made a loud clicking noise as the High Class loaded it and pointed it towards Sehseh again. "Goodbye little one."

There was a long, silent pause, then the High Class calmly dropped her stance, un-cocked her weapon and emptied the cartridges out, returning to a natural standing position with no expression in her eyes.

A sigh of relief came from behind and Alvin stepped around with a control panel in his hand. "Bloody hell, that was close."

Sehseh grinned and stood up far quicker than she should've. "I could have taken her down, you know."

"No, you couldn't," Alvin said, stepping closer. "You need..."

"Ladies and gentlemen," Iris' voice cut through as she stepped forward. "My security intel systems inform me that there is a large military force approaching the building with an ETA of one minute and thirty seconds."
Alvin paled and made a grab for Sehseh. "Right, time to go."
However, Sehseh side stepped up and looked up as a familiar sweeping brush was tossed down to her. Alvin blinked, "No way!"
Iris smiled as she walked past him, grinning in her own manic way. "What are you worried about?"
"She's injured, Stimmed up to high hell and is not going to go up against a PMC with you," Alvin virtually shouted, trying to grab for the pair. "It's suicide!"
Sehseh grinned wildly, letting out a high-pitched giggle as she started to skip away. "Yay! Lots of dust bunnies to play with! You coming, Iris?"
Iris smirked towards Sehseh. "Least number of kills has to clean the mansion?"

"Deal!" Sehseh said, rushing forward with Iris on her tail. "This is going to be fun."

"Too much fun," Iris replied, sounding just as gleeful.

35

5

GOO BUNNIES

Hundreds of rounds of bullets erupted through the night-time air, shooting forward into the door from the very moment that there was the merest vibration. The age-old stonework that had stood for centuries remained intact, whereas the wooden window frames disintegrated in a matter of seconds, the glass turning into lethal piles of glittering dust along with it. For a full minute, the barrage of bullets continued making their presence known, until the front of the vast old building looked like it had just been gutted by fire.

Finally, the Commander signalled for the guns to stop, and a harrowing silence crossed the courtyard. A car which had been unfortunately left out at the front was now barely even worth the price of a trip to the local scrap market, and the distinct smell of petrol lingered in the air.

Thankfully, no liquid fire rounds had been fired, but it was still a viable option.

For a long moment, no one dared to move or breath, as the faceless soldiers scanned the area for any signs of movement or indication of an attack coming their way.

The Commander knew that Battle Maids were tricky. He had personally seen the devastating effect that a squad of ten of them could do to a whole army. Even though they only had a limited intel on there being just two potential combatants, he was taking no chances, especially after reviewing security footage of the Special Classification Model.

She was an army in of herself, and a single-minded weapon. He had only heard rumours about the other combatant, and even the information that could be confirmed was rather sketchy, so for now, he just went with instinct. It had served him well and taking on Battle Maids was no easy feat.

There were still no signs of movement in the front of the house, and no alarms or sudden attackers appearing.

"Something's not right," one of the Captains muttered quietly over the radio, using a pair of heat and night vision binoculars to check all visible areas. "I'm not picking up anything at all... not even the parrot in the window is moving..."

A thought occurred to ask about that, since there shouldn't have been any animals in the building in the first place, but the faintest whistling noise happened to catch the attention of the Commander and he turned his head just in time to see a thin razor sharp wire cut across his neck as it scalped the Captain next to him with precision. At least twenty five others were taken out by the silent killer before the heads and shoulders began to roll on the ground and bodies collapsed to the floor.

"No fair!" Sehseh whined, glaring at Iris who had set the trap off. "You cheated!

"Did not," Iris replied back with a smirk, her eyes flashing towards the remaining PMC members who were clearly in a state of shock over everything. "But if you want, we can class this lot as one kill?"

Sehseh nodded, "Okay! That's fine by-" Sharply, she brought the sweeping brush head up and only slightly jolted back when a bullet landed in the end of it. "Oh, bunnies want to play?"

The man who had shot looked confused for a second before suddenly finding himself with a full body's worth of Maid as Sehseh ran and leapt at him, bringing the brush head around in a roundhouse motion. The bristles hardened into at least twenty sharp but thin knives that slammed into his chest, and tore through his armour like it was made of paper. The return swing tore skin from bones, and blood splattered everywhere around him, the scream cut off by death as the man slammed back against the ground.

Immediately two of his nearest comrades-in-arms leapt at Sehseh, one opening a full magazine of rifle bullets towards her whilst the second went for a stab towards her throat with his bayonet. The Maid was initially driven back by the bullets but used the bladed end of the brush to right herself up and grab hold of the bayonet when it was a mere inch away from her neck. She smiled sweetly towards the soldier, before throwing her full body into pushing back on the gun that was pointed at her. The man lost his balance, and Sehseh used the movement to jerk the weapon out of his hand, snap the bayonet cleanly off the barrel, and drop the gun to the ground. The bayonet ended up lodged in the throat of the one who had been shooting at her, whilst the end of the broom ended up in the first man's guts.

Pulling back with a spurt of blood from both men, Sehseh was quick to leap out of the way of another barrage of bullets that came her way as she made a large sweeping arch to the left. Too late did the group realise that she was building up speed and momentum for a long sweeping attack, but it was forgivable as they did have another problem to contend with.

Iris was tearing through the ranks of soldiers as if they were nothing more than rag dolls, appearing to casually flick her brightly coloured feather duster around. Each person that it came into contact with either exploded upon impact or was sliced and diced open in an ugly spray of limbs. One of the numerous masked men was able to avoid the duster and took a leap at her back, his arm going around her throat whilst he attempted to slam a blade into her side. It slid off the heavy armour of her dress without leaving so much as a scratch, and Iris merely reached over, grabbed the back of the man's head, and slammed him down onto the ground in front of her. Her dainty little shoe landed on his face, cracking the mask, and then proceeding through the rest of his face to leave nothing behind but a bloody mess of skin and bones.

She smirked towards a horrified solider who was about five feet away from her, clearly a rookie who had no idea of what he was dealing with in the slightest. "Eyes on the other one," Iris said. "She's more of a threat than me."

If the man spoke a word or made any indication of acknowledging the statement, Iris never knew, and she smartly ducked straight to the floor as the bladed broom swiped swiftly overhead. Sehseh was a blur of movement, leaping right then left, back and forth, swinging the deadly weapon with a precise and decisive movement that ended multiple lives in a few seconds.

Iris stood up and grinned towards her friend, giving her a thumbs up, before both Maids turned at the sound of the gates crashing open. A large tank with heavy double barrel guns had appeared and was clearly lining up its sights on the pair of them.

Sehseh turned towards Iris, almost bouncing with excitement. "Special Mode?"

The other Maid nodded, "It would seem to be the most appropriate." With the next blink of her eyes, they glowed a silver that matched the bangles on her arms, which also started to glow. The light was quick to engulf the Maid, and after a few seconds, it faded to reveal a fully armour-covered Maid that glimmered like she was made of liquid silver. Iris raised her hand and Sehseh tossed her the broom. As soon as it touched the other's hand, it vibrated and then expanded in a flurry of silver and glowing green and orange lights. Within the space of five seconds, it was a fully functional cannon gun with black rabbit artwork on the side of it.

The tank fired off a heavy ballistic round which roared past the two Maids as they dodged it, and it exploded into a fireball against the front of the ancient building.

"You missed us!" Sehseh called as she charged forward, drawing fire from a machine gun before dropping to the ground and skidding directly under the tank. Two knives appeared in her hands as she passed under, scraping loudly against the metal and cutting through everything that wasn't made of metal.

"All clear!" Sehseh called out once she was out from under the tank, and she rolled down into a virtually hidden ditch.

Iris fired at the tank. The projectile looked faintly like a purple mochi bunny rabbit sweet treat as it streamed through the air, before landing directly on top of the tank. For a second, there was only silence, before a high-pitched screech cut through the air, and a series of white hot electric lines came out of the projectile. The electricity engulfed the entire tank in a gigantic white bubble which then popped with a 'Chu' sound. All that was left behind was the original projectile, which flicked its purple ears, made another 'Chu' noise, and then leapt back into the gun like it was the most natural thing to do in the entire world.

The remaining PMC members stared at the Special as she turned towards them, sights locked on them, and then also noticed that Sehseh had stood up and was flanking them. They retreated even without the requested order, abandoning all weapons in the process.

"Don't go after them Sehseh," Iris called, as a small gun appeared, before spurting off a series of much smaller projectiles that were in the same style as the cannon gun but almost marble-sized in comparison. "These will take care of them."

Several globes of white engulfed the retreating men before disappearing with a series of pops, followed by lots of cute 'Chu' calls as the little beasts returned back to their mountings.

Sehseh smiled and clapped her hands, "I wish I could do something as cool as that."

Iris did not reply for a few seconds, the glow engulfing her once again, but she smiled towards Sehseh, "You really don't, it's a drain on...hey!"

Sehseh blinked and didn't get a chance to register what Iris was reacting to. A fist—small, dainty and perfect—suddenly slammed into the back of her head. Stars immediately appeared in front of her eyes and were quickly replaced by tons of code that scrambled across in red, green, and blue lettering as a sudden hotness shot through her entire body.

"Maybe you'll remember me now, Seraphina," a voice said, feminine and vaguely familiar, before blackness took hold of Sehseh, and she crashed down towards the ground.

Iris fired several charges towards the two girls standing in the gateway, unable to believe that they had completely forgotten about the two kittens from inside. They both jumped out of the way, then disappeared with a touch of a button. Iris cursed whoever had created the teleportation technology and ran towards Sehseh, who was lying still on the ground.

"No!" she half wailed. "No, no, no... Sehseh, come on, wake up!"

Sehseh didn't move, but there was code flashing across her eyes as something deep inside her began to stir.

つづく

Tsudzuku
To Be Continued

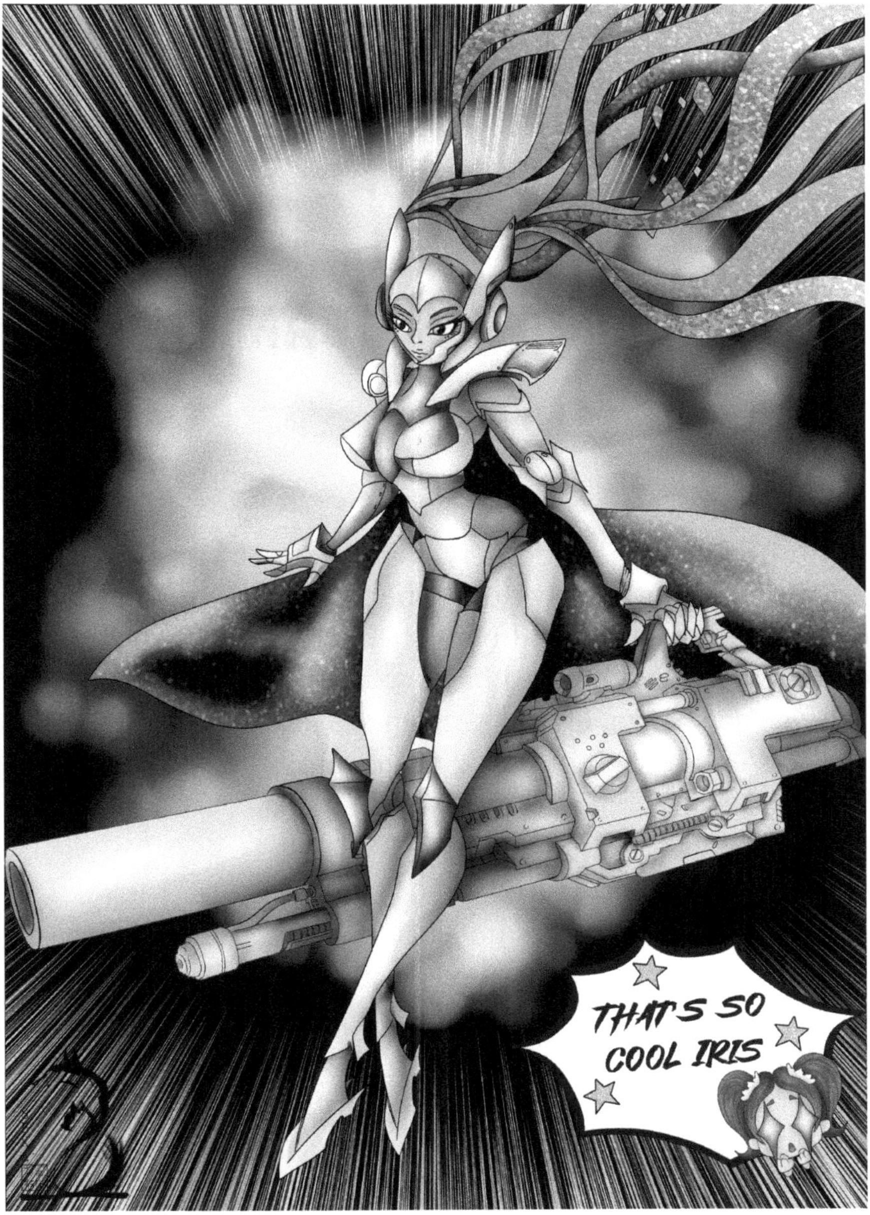
THAT'S SO COOL IRIS

6

CREATIVE TEAM

Author - Sarah Elliot
An geek who got to writing when she was ten after finding out she was dsylexic and built this crazy world with Kurt. Is currently at the other end of the country, running free in the valleys and soaking up the sunshine. Is also working on future projects linked and not linked to this project so do keep up to date via socials or just to give Wolfie an hug.

Co-Creator - Kurt Dalton
Still believes that he's not really necessary to the project, even though he literally helped create everything and inspired several of the other related works which are in developement. As well as put up with the earliest drafts of this madness to point out various bits and come up with more insane ideas - yes a lot of them weren't used but we can reporpous them later I'm sure.

Artist - Katrina Allcroft
Has been drawing, painting and creating for many numerous years and does do commisions if anyone is interested or looking for work. Came on board to draw stuff and still gets

annoyed at the authors descriptions of clothes sometimes as 'is her dress v-lined, sweetheart style or other.

Editor - Boo Lai

We're pretty sure is a cat who lives in a human body and does her own thing. Resurfaces to put red splotches over the work and then disappears again.

Milton Keynes UK
Ingram Content Group UK Ltd.
UKHW022334050624
443649UK00017BA/1066

9 781739 333645